The Story of
SANTA CLAUS

By Barbara Shook Hazen
Illustrated by Carolyn Bracken

A GOLDEN BOOK • NEW YORK
Western Publishing Company, Inc., Racine, Wisconsin 53404

MCMXCIV

Claus was born long ago on a brrrrishly bone-freezing
Christmas Eve. Outside, it was so cold that the cottage was buried
in snow. Inside, it was so cold that the Christmas tree was covered
with icicles.

From the day he was born, little Claus far preferred cold to
cozy, unlike his brother, Cloyd, and his sister, Clara, who liked warm
and sunny.

"Oh, woe and worry," his mother exclaimed each time she found
little Claus uncovered in his crib. "You'll catch your comeuppance
of sneezes and wheezes."

But little Claus never did. Instead, he grew red-cheeked, round,
and jolly. He was a fat, happy baby. What made him happiest was to
toss off his bedcovers, wriggle out of his nightshirt, and chuckle,
"Ho, ho, ho!"

Nicely, icily cold was the way he liked to be.

As soon as he could walk little Claus went outside to play. He liked the feel of fresh, freezing air. Indoor heat gave him the itchy prickles. But Cloyd and Clara preferred to stay inside, with cups of steaming hot cocoa and all their indoor toys.

His mother always worried that he would get lost in the snow. So she bundled him in a bright red snowsuit with fuzzy white trim. Red made little Claus easier to see in the snow. Then she gave him a kiss and pinned his house key to his sleeve.

"Oh, woe and worry. If you only like snow, what will become of you when you are big?" she fretted.

"Something good. Ho, ho, ho! Someday you'll see," little Claus always answered with a merry twinkle in his eye.

Little Claus's favorite playthings were ice and snow. He made amazing ice-block castles, snow sculptures, and toys. The only trouble was, they always melted when he tried to take them inside.

One problem little Claus had was losing his house key. One day, during his fun and frolic with the reindeer that lived in the woods, the key fell off his sleeve. When it was time to come in for supper, the house key was lost somewhere in the snow.

Little Claus looked, and looked, and looked, but he couldn't find his key in the deep drifts of snow. Claus knew his mother wouldn't mind if he knocked, but he was a quiet boy and didn't want to disturb her. So he thought of a way to get in by himself, without the key. It was a way that was thoughtful as well as clever.

He taught himself to climb the slippery icicles up, up, up to the cottage rooftop. Then he let himself in by clambering down the chimney.

From then on he always landed in the fireplace with a *clatter-pop!,* a sack full of fine fresh snowballs, and a happy "Ho, ho, ho! Here I am! And look what I have for you."

Also unlike his brother and sister, little Claus was shy, especially in front of strangers.

Cloyd and Clara loved to sing and dance and recite in front of an audience. They thrived on attention and applause. But little Claus preferred to stay unseen. When Cloyd and Clara performed, he crouched behind the window curtains in the nice cold draft.

When everyone left, he emerged with a happy "Ho, ho, ho! Here I am. And thank you for the show."

But the biggest difference between Claus and his brother and sister was that, unlike them, he far preferred giving to getting.

Giving put the spring in his step, the sweet in his smile. Giving made little Claus happier than anything, even eating ice cream.

Cloyd and Clara liked getting. No matter what they had, they wanted more, more, more—more toys, more treats, more turns. Most of all, each wanted more than the other.

Little Claus always gave them whatever they wanted. When Cloyd said, "Give me your purple crayon, I want it now!" little Claus would say, "I'm glad you want it. Here, please have it."

When Clara said, "Give me your jack-in-the-box, or else," little Claus said, "Ho, ho, ho! Here it is. Now what else can I give you?"

Soon his heart was full, but his toy shelf was as bare as a winter branch.

One year on his birthday little Claus gave away all his presents, as well as the corner pieces of birthday cake with the sugary icing roses.

This made his mother so happy that she hugged little Claus and called him "a little saint, my little Santa Claus." She told Cloyd and Clara that they should try to be more like "dear, sweet Santa Claus."

This made Cloyd and Clara jealous and furious. "Just you wait," they hissed while trying to kick their little brother under the table.

As he got bigger his giving got Claus into bigger trouble. Cloyd and Clara got sick and tired of hearing about how good Claus was, especially compared to them.

They tried to make Claus's life miserable. They were surly and snitty. They stuck out their tongues at Claus when their mother wasn't looking.

They teased young Claus with singsong rhymes like "Goody-goody Santa Claus, we don't like you BECAUSE," and "No one likes you, Santa Claus, we all wish you'd just get lost."

Cloyd and Clara played mean tricks on Claus, too. They put knots in his snowsuit sleeves, glue on his sled, and melted his ice castles. They even tucked hot potatoes between his bedsheets. They knew how he hated anything hot.

The meaner they were, the more their mother said, "Oh, woe and worry, why can't you be more like dear, sweet Santa Claus?"

His giving also got young Claus in trouble at school.

He gave away all his school books, including the ones with his homework inside. He gave away his pencil box and his hockey stick.

Every school morning Claus put everything he had in the *GIVE* bag by the front door.

Every lunchtime Claus gave away all his food. He gave his porridge to a little boy and his sandwich to a little girl. He gave his carrot sticks to the reindeer living in the woods nearby.

But the one thing Claus always saved was his apple. He saved it for his teacher. While the others were eating, Claus sneaked back to his classroom and left the apple on his teacher's desk. He was too shy to give it to her himself.

When his teacher saw the apple, she was delighted. She looked down and saw the snowy footprints leading out the door and guessed who had been there. "Such a dear, sweet Santa Claus," she said with a smile.

One day Burley Bigmouth, the class bully, saw Claus put the apple on the teacher's desk.

"Teacher's pet," Burley snorted. He told the others, "We've got to get that teacher's pet. And I have an idea how."

That afternoon Burley and his buddies waited for young Claus after school. They waited behind a snowbank with a huge pile of hard-packed snowballs.

When Claus came by, whistling, they aimed and fired, pelting him.

"Ho, ho, ho!" cried young Claus, grinning happily, as he jumped and dodged around the icy snowballs. "Ice and snow's the way to go."

Then one day, when Claus was big enough to be home alone, the worst happened.

A peddler with a wagon and a sly look came to the cottage door. "Have you anything to give?" he asked. "My name's Jake, and my motto is, You give, I take."

"Take all and anything you want, Jake," Claus said cheerfully. "Here, I'll help you carry everything out."

Claus gave Jake all the food that was in the cupboard, plus all the fruit and eggs, and even his mother's fresh-baked cherry pie.

He gave Jake all the clothes in the closets. He gave him the bedding, the beds, and all the chairs.

He was in the middle of giving Jake all of Cloyd's and Clara's toys, games, and puzzles when they returned home with their mother.

"Ho, ho, ho! Glad to be of help," Claus said with a smile as his horrified brother and sister ran up the walk.

"No, no, no! Claus has got to go!" Clara shrieked as she ran after Jake and all her precious belongings.

"See," Cloyd said, turning to their mother. "That's what comes of giving. It gets you nowhere and nothing."

"Oh, worry and woe, what will we do?" their mother wailed.

"Uh-oh, I don't know," Claus said sadly. And for the first time ever he frowned.

Claus was still frowning when Clara came back with Jake, who promised to put everything back in return for one more cherry pie.

While his mother baked and Cloyd and Clara brought their things inside, Claus thought and thought.

Suddenly his face broke into a smile as bright as sunshine after a summer shower.

"I've got it!" Claus said happily. "I'll do what's best for all of us. I'll go away—far, far away. I'll settle someplace where it's nicely icy all the time. I'm almost grown. I'm even beginning to get a beard. I'm big enough to be out on my own."

"More woe and worry," Claus's mother said with tears in her eyes. "I'll worry that you won't be happy. Besides, what will you do?"

"I'll do what I do best," Claus told his mother. "I'll set up a workshop. I'll make toys and things to give away, because giving is what I like to do best.

"And every year on *my* birthday—on Christmas Eve—I'll come back and bring *you* presents," Claus said. "That way you'll know I love you. And you'll see how happy I am."

"Goody!" cried Clara. She clapped her hands and said, "I'll give you a list of all the stuff I want!"

"Me, too, me, too!" Cloyd shouted, pushing his sister aside.

"Ho, ho, ho! There will be plenty for everybody," Claus said as he gave them a big hug.

Claus left a few months later. He left after building a sturdy sled and after training Dasher and Prancer, his favorite reindeer, to pull it so swiftly that it seemed to fly.

He left wearing the new red snowsuit his mother had made. It had extra-thick fuzz on the collar and cuffs, and a woolly stocking cap with a jaunty white pom-pom.

Before he left, his mother pinned the house key to his sleeve, kissed him, and said, "Don't lose this and do come back. I'll miss you, Santa Claus. And I will worry."

"Don't forget anything on my list," Cloyd and Clara said.

"I won't forget anything and please don't worry," Claus said with a smile. "What I will do will make everybody happy. Believe me, you'll see."

Then chuckling and crying, "Ho, ho, ho! Go, Dasher! Go, Prancer!" young Claus took off in a whirl of snow.

As Cloyd and Clara watched him disappear into the sky, they began to remember how nice Claus had always been to them. Then they remembered how meanly they had treated him. Clara's eyes filled with tears. Cloyd looked down at his feet and kicked the snow. They were starting to miss him already.

As Claus traveled north the air got nicely icy. The wind whistled and he whistled along with it.

Soon there were no houses or towns or people. There was snow and ice as far as the eye could see.

Then, over a snowy hill, Claus was surprised to see smoke. He followed the smoke to a cluster of quaint cottages. In the middle of the cottages was a red-and-white pole. It looked like a candy cane with a ball on top.

"I wonder what it is?" Claus said to himself, scratching his beard.

"It means you're at the North Pole, a glad and giving place," a voice squeaked. The voice belonged to a little old elf with pointed ears, a peaked cap, and a squinty smile.

"I'm called Santa Claus, and I'm a giving person myself," Santa told the elf. "I like to make things to give to others. This looks like just the kind of place for me to settle down and set up a workshop. Maybe you could help me."

As Santa spoke a gaggle of elves scampered out of their cottages. "Hurray!" they all shouted, tossing their funny little caps in the air. "We've never had a workshop. Now we can give more than ever before! When do we start?"

The elves gave Santa their guest cottage to stay in. It had
icicles on all the windows and was comfortably cool and suited
him perfectly.

Then they built a wonderful toy workshop for Santa. In it
was everything they needed to make every kind of toy from
old-fashioned to newfangled. As soon as their workshop was
finished, the clever elves started helping to make all the things on
Cloyd's and Clara's lists.

They tested the toys, too. Toy testing was one of the best parts of
toy making.

Months passed, and the elves loved their work so much that they couldn't stop. They made plenty of extra toys and presents. There were so many gifts that the elves had to sew a special sack to put everything in,

and build a bigger sleigh as well.

They also had to train six more reindeer to pull it. The magical elves even taught the reindeer how to fly by using their antlers to lift off and their hooves to paw the air and steer.

By the time Santa Claus was ready to go, the cold air had turned his beard as white as the snow he loved so much.

Finally, on Christmas Eve, the elves helped Santa fill his sack and pack the sleigh.

"Good-bye, much joy and safe landings!" they cried, waving their caps as Santa Claus took off.

Guided by the stars, Santa steered the sleigh through the clear night sky, over clouds, trees, and towns, till he hovered over the cottage where he was born.

That was when he reached for his house key and realized he'd lost it, just as he had when he was little.

So he landed on the roof, slung his sack over his shoulder, and slid down the chimney, just the way he had when he was little.

"Ho, ho, ho! Here I am!" Santa Claus chuckled merrily as he appeared in the fireplace.

"Good-bye, worry and woe," Santa's mother said as soon as she saw him. "You look wonderfully happy, and that makes me happy. I won't ever have to worry anymore."

Cloyd and Clara jumped up and hugged their brother. They didn't say, "Where are our presents?" or sing nasty rhymes, or stick out their tongues.

Instead, Clara said, "I missed you a lot, and I have something for you. Jingle bells for your sleigh, so we can hear you when you come next time."

"I've gotten to like giving, too," Cloyd said. "And I have something for you. I made the cookies myself and the milk is nicely, icily cold, just the way you like it."

"Thank you," Santa Claus said happily. Then he tucked the presents under the tree and they all celebrated.

Late that night, after they had opened their presents, Santa looked at his family and sighed. "It's been great seeing all of you, but now it's time for me to get back to the North Pole so I can get to work again," he said.

Then he looked at the piles of unopened gifts and added, "Oh, me, oh, my, why didn't you open the rest of your presents?"

"I have plenty right now," Clara said. "I have my skates and my tool box."

"Don't give them to me," Cloyd added. "I have my guitar and my puzzle game."

"But the very best gift was having you come home again," they said together.

"It certainly was," Santa's mother agreed. "Your visit perked me up more than a spring tonic."

"Ho, ho, ho! I'm glad," Santa said with a merry grin.

Then he hugged his family and said, "I'll be back next year, and every year after. Write me at the North Pole if there's anything that you want."

He left with his sack and a cheery "Merry Christmas! And a Happy New Year, too!"

And as he left he had a wonderful idea.

"Ho, ho, ho! I know what I'll do with all those presents," Santa said to his reindeer. "I'll deliver them to children all over the world. Now, isn't that a good idea!"

The reindeer nodded their approval, and Santa climbed into the sleigh. Once again they soared into the crisp night sky.

On his way, Santa stopped everywhere children lived, from Timbuktu to Kalamazoo, from Nome to Paris to East Harris.

The more places Santa went, and the more presents he tucked under Christmas trees, the happier he became.

But none of the children saw Santa Claus. He sneaked in, in his special Santa way, because he was still very shy.

The most any child heard was the faint tinkle of a jingle bell or the tap of a reindeer hoof up on the roof.

By the time Santa reached the North Pole, his sack was empty, it was Christmas morning, and he was bursting his snowsuit buttons with joy—the joy of Christmas giving.

Many years have passed since Santa Claus's first visit to the children of the world on Christmas Eve. But every year he comes as he promised and delivers the presents he and his elves have been working on all year at the North Pole workshop.

Santa loves children and he loves making them happy. Except for a little more white in his beard and a little more bright in his smile, Santa hasn't changed. He still likes cold better than cozy, and he's still very shy. But, above all, Santa still prefers giving to getting.

You may not see Santa Claus on Christmas Eve, but on Christmas morning you'll know he was there. You'll know when you see the presents he's left under the tree and you feel a happy "Ho, ho, ho!" in your own heart.